Please visit our website, www.garethstevens.com. For a free color catalog of all our high-quality books, call toll free 1-800-542-2595 or fax 1-877-542-2596.

Library of Congress Cataloging-in-Publication Data

Jeffries, Joyce.
 Hot and cold / Joyce Jeffries.
     pages cm. — (Dinosaur school)
 ISBN 978-1-4339-8092-3 (paperback)
 ISBN 978-1-4339-8093-0 (6-pack)
 ISBN 978-1-4339-8091-6 (library binding)
 1. Heat—Juvenile literature. 2. Cold—Juvenile literature. 3. Polarity—Juvenile literature. I. Title.
 QC256.J44 2013
 536—dc23

                                        2012023550

First Edition

Published in 2013 by
Gareth Stevens Publishing
111 East 14th Street, Suite 349
New York, NY 10003

Designer: Mickey Harmon
Editor: Katie Kawa

All illustrations by Planman Technologies

Printed in the United States of America

CPSIA compliance information: Batch #CW13GS: For further information contact Gareth Stevens, New York, New York at 1-800-542-2595.

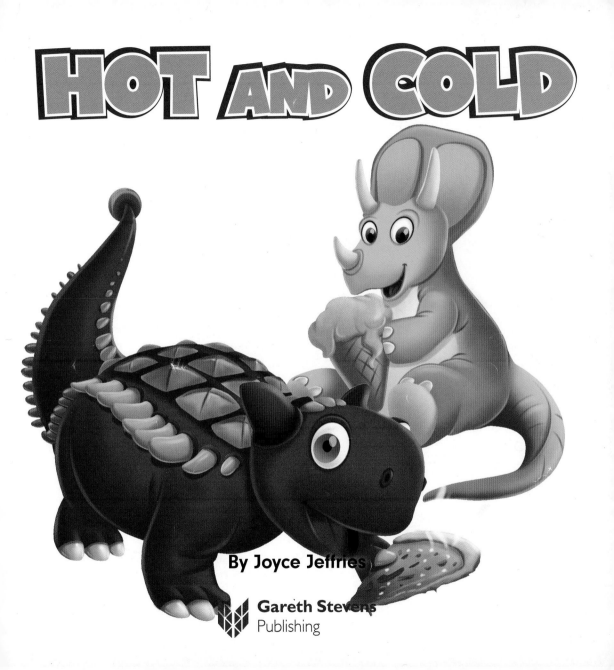

HOT AND COLD

By Joyce Jeffries

Gareth Stevens
Publishing

Some things are hot.

4

Some things are cold.

The sun is hot.

6

The snow is cold.

The pizza is hot.

The ice cream is cold.

9

The fire is hot.

The ice is cold.

The cocoa is hot.

The milk is cold.

The oven is hot.

The freezer is cold.

The soup is hot.

The juice is cold.

The summer is hot.

I wear shorts in the summer.

The winter is cold.

I wear a coat in the winter.

What do you do
when it is hot?

What do you do
when it is cold?

Hot and Cold

HOT	COLD	HOT	COLD
 sun	snow	oven	freezer
pizza	ice cream	soup	juice
fire	ice	summer	winter
cocoa	milk		

24